The Kingdom of Wrenly

of

Wrenly

12

The Sorcerer's Shadow

By Jordan Quinn

Illustrated by Robert McPhillips

LITTLE SIMON

New York London Toronto Sydney New Delhi

LITTLE SIMON
An imprint of Simon & Schuster Children's Publishing Division
1230 Avenue of the Americas, New York, New York 10020
First Little Simon hardcover edition September 2017
Copyright © 2017 by Simon & Schuster, Inc.
Also available in a Little Simon paperback edition.
All rights reserved, including the right of reproduction in whole or in part in any form.
LITTLE SIMON is a registered trademark of Simon & Schuster, Inc.,
and associated colophon is a trademark of Simon & Schuster, Inc.
For information about special discounts for bulk purchases, please contact
Simon & Schuster Special Sales at 1-866-506-1949 or business@simonandschuster.com.
The Simon & Schuster Speakers Bureau can bring authors to your live event.
For more information or to book an event contact the Simon & Schuster Speakers Bureau
at 1-866-248-3049 or visit our website at www.simonspeakers.com.
Manufactured in the United States of America 1020 MTN
6 8 10 9 7
This book has been cataloged with the Library of Congress.
ISBN 978-1-5344-0000-9 (hc)
ISBN 978-1-4814-9999-6 (pbk)
ISBN 978-1-5344-0001-6 (eBook)

CONTENTS

CHAPTER 1

The Rider

Dudda-lump!
  Dudda-lump!
  Dudda-lump!

Horse hooves drummed frantically across the forest floor. Prince Lucas, Clara, and Ruskin stopped to listen. Lucas had just rescued a nest of baby birds that had fallen from a tree. He gently rested the nest in the crook of a thick branch so the mother

bird would find her babies safe and sound. Then he climbed down the tree and jumped to the ground. The pounding hooves drew closer.

"Someone sure is in a huge hurry," Lucas remarked as he looked down the trail. "I wonder if something's wrong."

The rider roared into view and thundered right by them. Lucas and Clara had to shield their faces from the dirt kicked up by the rider.

"It's a knight!" Clara exclaimed.

Lucas nodded. "He's probably headed for the castle," he said. "Let's follow him!"

Ruskin, Lucas's dragon, took flight. The two best friends jumped on their horses and galloped after the rider, who had ridden far ahead. Lucas and Clara slowed to a canter when they got to the village. The villagers had spilled into the street

4

to see who was in such a big rush. The butcher, the blacksmith, and the chandler had all left their shops and were standing in the midst of a crowd. They watched through the churned-up dust that the rider had left in his wake.

Clara waved to her father as they sped past her family's bakery, the Daily Bread.

"What's going on, Clara?" her father asked.

"I don't know," she called over her shoulder. "But we're going to find out!"

The children weaved in and out of the crowd and rode on to the castle. When they reached the front gate, the rider had just tied his horse to the royal hitching post. He approached the castle guards and pulled off his helmet.

A cascade of dark brown hair tumbled over the knight's shoulders.

Lucas cupped his hand over his mouth.

The rider was a *girl*!

CHAPTER 2

Trouble in Trellis

Clara jabbed Lucas in the side with her elbow. "Don't look so surprised!" she said angrily. "Girls make excellent knights."

Lucas rubbed his side where he'd been hit. "Ow," he said. "I'm sorry. It's just that you don't see lady knights every day in the kingdom of Wrenly." Then he thought about it and added, "But that should change."

Clara unfolded her arms. "Yes, I am certain it will," she agreed, and the smile returned to her face.

Then they crept closer to hear what the knight had to say.

"My name is Dame Laurel of Trellis," she said. Dame Laurel's armor was made completely of things found in the forest. She had on a breastplate of hawthorn leaves dipped in bronze and a helmet and shield made of hickory wood. "I have an urgent message for the king."

Lucas and Clara gave each other a look.

"What could be so urgent?" Clara whispered.

Lucas shrugged.

They hitched their horses and followed the castle guards and Dame Laurel into the castle. The guards sent a message to the king. Soon they escorted Dame Laurel into the king's special meeting chamber.

Lucas and Clara hid behind a purple curtain just outside the grand room and eavesdropped.

"State your case," they heard King Caleb say.

Dame Laurel bowed before the king.

"There's been unrest in Trellis, Your Majesty," the knight announced. "It began when a farmer's herd of cattle was frightened into a stampede. The cows haven't returned."

The king stroked his bristly blond beard. "Runaway cows?" he questioned. "That hardly seems a matter for the king's court."

Dame Laurel bowed her head respectfully.

"There's more, Your Highness," she said. "The forest creatures are behaving strangely. The bears have left their dens. The beavers have stopped working. The frogs no longer croak, and the mother birds have abandoned their nests."

Lucas poked Clara. "I wonder if that's what happened to the baby birds we rescued this afternoon?" he whispered.

Clara's eyes widened. "It must be!" she whispered back.

They peeked through the curtain to learn more.

"What do you think this is all about?" asked the king.

A grave look came over Dame

Laurel's face. "Your Majesty, I believe it may be sorcery," she said.

The king shifted uncomfortably in his bejeweled chair. "Then I will appoint a team to help you investigate this matter immediately," he declared. "The team must leave first thing in the morning. If what you say is true, we can't afford to wait."

Dame Laurel thanked the king as the guards escorted her to a guest chamber.

Lucas and Clara slipped out from behind the curtain, walked casually

through the great hall, and then hurried outside.

"We have to find a way to join the king's team," Lucas said.

"I know," Clara said. "Maybe we can entice your father with something from my family's bakery. The king loves sweets, and I know just the thing. . . ."

A sly smile spread over Lucas's face. "Perfect."

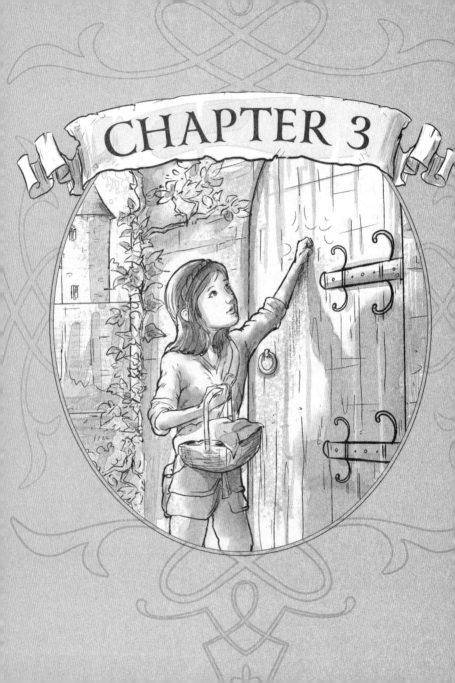

CHAPTER 3

Sir Desdan's Team

Tap!

  Tap!

  Tap!

Clara knocked on the castle's kitchen door at seven o'clock in the morning, the time King Caleb and Queen Tasha always had breakfast. A basket of cinnamon rolls with sweet vanilla glaze—the king's favorite—hung from her wrist.

"Perfect timing," Lucas whispered as he let Clara in. He had been waiting in the kitchen for her arrival. "My mother and father just sat down."

Clara followed Lucas through the kitchen and into the dining room.

"You're going to put me out of a job," grumbled Cook as they walked past.

Clara tried not to laugh.

Lucas pushed open the dining room door.

"Clara has something special for you," Lucas announced.

Clara stepped forward and held out her basket of cinnamon rolls for King Caleb. The king smiled and lifted the napkin from the basket. Then he rubbed his hands together excitedly.

"Oh, my favorite!" he cried, and he placed a warm cinnamon roll on his plate. He licked the glaze from his fingers. "Scrumptious! And now that you two have my attention, what is it you want?"

Clara shot a glance at Lucas. Had the cinnamon rolls plan been *that* obvious? Lucas drew in a breath and got to the point.

"We'd like to go on the mission to Trellis," he said.

The king held a bite of cinnamon roll on the end of his fork. "Oh, you would, would you?" he said.

Lucas and Clara sat at the table, and Lucas stated his case.

"Father, if I'm going to be king someday, I need to understand

the mysteries of our kingdom," he argued. "How else will I become a good ruler?"

His father's smile seemed to say, *Such a grown-up boy!* Then the king looked at his wife, who also smiled knowingly.

"Okay," the king said. "But if we let you go, you must be very alert.

Sorcery can be extremely dangerous." Then the king turned to Clara. "And you, fair maiden, may join Lucas if your family allows."

Clara nodded gratefully. Her parents had already given her permission to go. She had asked when they were baking the cinnamon rolls early in the morning.

"Sir Desdan is in charge of the mission," the king went on. "You two must do exactly as he says."

"Ugh," Lucas said.

Sir Desdan was his least favorite knight. He was plenty noble, but he was also a bit of a grump.

"I will, Father," Lucas promised as he gulped down his milk and grabbed a roll for the road.

Then Lucas and Clara raced to the stables to saddle their horses and meet the rest of the team. Ruskin followed close behind. The other knights, including Dame Laurel, had already mounted their horses.

"Prince Lucas and Clara Gills here. We are reporting for duty by order of the king!" Lucas said.

Sir Desdan was a bearded knight with dark, wavy hair. He looked down his nose at the children and Ruskin. "Oh great!" he grumbled. "Since when is babysitting children one of my knightly duties?"

Lucas put his hands on his hips. "We do not need a babysitter," he said curtly. "We're here to help by order of the crown."

Sir Desdan shifted in his saddle. "If you ride with us, then you must follow all my commands," he said gruffly and yanked the reins.

Lucas and Clara mounted their horses.

"Yes, sir," Lucas agreed through gritted teeth. He didn't like to take orders from someone who showed him such little respect. The prince had more than proved his worthiness on many a mission.

Clara pulled up alongside Lucas. "Simmer down," she whispered.

Lucas snapped the reins. "When the time is right, we'll show him what *children* can do!"

CHAPTER 4

Shaking Like a Leaf

Lucas and Clara galloped alongside the team of knights into the forest of Trellis.

"Be on the lookout for anything unusual," Dame Laurel called to the others.

Not far into the woods Ruskin got spooked. *That's odd,* Lucas thought. *I wonder what scared him.* The young dragon flew to the safety of his

master and landed on the back of Lucas's horse.

"What's wrong?" Lucas called over his shoulder.

Ruskin whimpered and leaned in close against Lucas's back. *Does Ruskin sense something we can't see?* the prince wondered.

Lucas scanned the forest again. Everything seemed normal to him except that he did not see any sign of villagers or homes. Where was Trellis, anyway?

"Look at the trees!" Clara cried suddenly. "There's something wrong about the way the leaves are blow-ing. They are moving in the opposite direction of the wind."

Sir Desdan looked at the trees and roared with laughter. "You're right! The leaves are shaking in the breeze—shaking like scared little children!" he mocked. Then he laughed even harder.

Lucas and Clara looked at each other and shook their heads in disgust.

"But Clara is *right*!" Dame Laurel shouted over the beating hooves. "The wind is blowing into our faces, but the leaves are blowing as if the wind is coming from behind us."

Sir Desdan pulled on the reins and came to a stop. The other riders slowed to a stop too. Then the know-it-all knight placed his pointer finger in his mouth, pulled it out, and stuck it in the air. He frowned. Sure enough, the wind was blowing toward them, but the leaves were blowing in the opposite direction.

Lucas trotted close to Sir Desdan. "When the leaves don't obey the wind, it means something has gone terribly wrong."

Sir Desdan scowled at the prince. "Anyone knows that," he said sharply.

Lucas flicked the reins and picked up the trail behind Dame Laurel. He didn't want to be anywhere near that uppity knight.

Soon Dame Laurel stopped in front of an enormous oak tree. Etched into the side of the trunk was a great arched double door. She reached into her saddle and pulled out a white horn. Raising it to her lips, she blew into it, and a mighty bellow echoed through the forest. A moment later the doors slowly creaked open.

Dame Laurel waved the knights inside. They entered the tree on horseback. Then the doors closed behind them, and all at once it was pitch-dark.

"I apologize," Dame Laurel said.

"The torch is out. Just sit tight."

The ground began to rumble and shake beneath them.

Clip-clop! Clip-clop! The horses struggled to keep their balance.

The team of knights was lifted through the hollow of the tree.

"The floor is moving!" Lucas whispered.

And, slowly, up they went.

CHAPTER 5

Bully Beware

When the doors opened again, everyone stared in wonder. Before the knights stood Trellis, an entire city built in the midst of the treetops!

A castle made of hand-carved wood, with many towers, stood in the center of Trellis. The top of each tower had the dental work of a jack-'o-lantern smile with every other tooth missing. Spires shingled in bark pointed to the sky. Everything had been built with things found in the forest.

Tree houses lined the village streets. Some had a branch growing right through the middle of the home. All the houses had flower boxes that spilled over with colorful blooms. Everything in the city was connected by bridges and wooden walkways. Street vendors sold nuts, berries, and vegetables along the sides.

Lucas whistled in wonder. "Trellis is magical," he commented. "Like the world's biggest tree fort."

Sir Desdan rolled his eyes to let Lucas know his comment was childish and unknightly.

But Dame Laurel winked at the children. "Trellis is enchanting."

She led the team to the castle, where they each had a room. The knights settled in to rest for tomorrow's mission. But Lucas, Clara, and Ruskin set out to explore the village.

As they walked along the bridges and walkways, they heard a ruckus up ahead. Two kids had tripped another boy, who tumbled into a fruit cart, knocking it over. Strawberries, blueberries, and blackberries speckled the road.

The fruit vendor scolded the boy on the ground for ruining his fruit. This made the bullies howl with laughter, and they ran off, slapping each other's hands.

The prince ran to the boy's side and offered to help him. The boy grabbed hold of Lucas and stood up.

"Are you okay?" Lucas asked.

"Yes," the boy said. "My friends like to joke around. Sometimes the joke goes too far."

"That's not how friends act where we are from," said Clara. "I'm Clara. This is Lucas, and this is Ruskin."

The boy gave a nervous smile. "A

dragon? Wow. Oh, I am Petros."

Petros had large brown eyes and shaggy black hair that fell over his large ears, hiding them from the world.

Lucas and Clara helped him pick up the mess.

"Thank you," Petros said. "May I

return the favor? You must be new to Trellis. I could show you the city."

Lucas handed a gold coin to the vendor to pay for the spoiled fruit. "Thanks, but we have to return to the castle for dinner. We're here on official business for my father, the king of Wrenly."

Petros bowed when
he heard Lucas was a
prince. Then his face
darkened slightly.
"What brings
you to Trellis, then?"

Lucas shook his
head slowly. "I'm afraid
that information is top secret,"
he said. "Thank you for the offer,
though. Another time."

Then Lucas bowed, and Petros
left them with a wave. Ruskin,
though, gave a small whimper as
the boy disappeared.

CHAPTER 6

Not Fair!

Lucas gazed out of his window and shivered. A thick blanket of fog had settled over Trellis. *Wow,* Lucas thought. *You can't see anything!* He changed into his clothes, slipped on his boots, and hurried to meet the others in the dining room.

At breakfast Clara and Lucas ate steaming bowls of oatmeal. They both drizzled honey and sprinkled

blueberries on top. Then the team
mapped out a plan for the day.

"With the heavy fog, the visibility
is very low," Sir Desdan noted.

Dame Laurel set down her spoon.
"Dense fog is very unusual in Trellis.
I have reason to believe there's some-
thing sinister behind it."

Sir Desdan brought his fist down on the table, and the knights all flinched.

"Well, that settles it," he said. "We can't have these younglings along if we're really dealing with sorcery."

Lucas pushed back his chair, and it scraped over the stone floor so hard, the sound echoed throughout the entire dining room. "You can't leave us behind," he cried. "My father wants us to be part of this mission. It's by *order of the king*."

Sir Desdan shook his head firmly. "And the king also said you must follow my orders. This mission is dangerous, and I can't let anything happen to the prince or the prince's friend."

Both Lucas and Clara huffed in disgust.

"We've been on missions far more dangerous than this," Lucas argued.

Sir Desdan stood up from the table. "The answer is *no*," he boomed. "You're to stay behind, and that's an *order*."

Ruskin growled.

"And call off that pesky dragon of yours," he added. Then Sir Desdan snapped his fingers, and the knights followed him to the stables.

"I'm sorry," Dame Laurel said before leaving. "Sir Desdan is harsh, but it's probably safer this way."

Lucas threw his napkin onto the table. "This is *so* unfair."

Clara rested her hand on the prince's shoulder. "It is, but have we ever let anyone stop us before?"

Lucas looked at Clara thought-fully. "You're right. And we won't let them stop us this time, either."

CHAPTER 7

Magical
Mystery Tour

Lucas and Clara wandered the foggy streets of Trellis in search of strange things, while Ruskin refused to leave the castle. The dragon was disturbed by the unnatural weather.

"How are we going to find any clues in this?" Lucas asked, brushing away the mist as if it were cobwebs.

"Maybe the fog *is* one of our clues," Clara said. "What in all of Wrenly could cause such strange weather?"

Lucas turned in a circle, listening for the sounds of the city.

"You know what else is odd?" he said. "I can't hear any street noise. I don't think there's anybody out here today except us. Maybe Ruskin was smart to stay behind."

No sooner had Lucas spoken those words than somebody bumped into Clara.

"Sorry," said a boy's voice.

Clara recognized the shadowy outline of shaggy hair. "Petros!" she cried.

Petros squinted through the fog. "My friends from yesterday!" he exclaimed. Then he looked down at his feet in shame. "Oh no. Now I've hurt even those who were nice to me."

Lucas patted Petros on the back. "It's not your fault. It's this fog."

Clara laughed. "Lucas is right. I can barely see my hand when I hold it out in front of me."

Petros smiled, and as he did the fog began to lift. The storefronts and tree houses became visible again.

"How's your mission going?" he asked.

Lucas frowned. "We had to stay here. The head knight thought it was too dangerous for children. Even Ruskin decided to stay at the castle."

Petros nodded sympathetically. "If you are free, then shall I show you around Trellis?"

Lucas and Clara looked at each other and nodded.

"We'd love that!" the prince said.

Petros escorted Lucas and Clara to the playground first. Zip lines connected one tree to another. Slides zigzagged down and around the tree trunks, like the marble runways the prince built in his playroom. At the bottom of every chute there was a

ladder to climb back to the top. The playground was full of kids now that the fog had cleared.

When the kids saw Petros, they started shouting taunts at him:

"Oh great, it's Bad Luck Petros."

"Get out of here, you clumsy oaf, before you break the whole playground!"

"Yeah, we're trying to have a good time here."

As Petros stepped forward, some of the children ran away.

He clenched his fists and his face turned a raging shade of red.

The sky above them grew dark again with clouds that swirled angrily. Lucas and Clara thought a mighty storm was about to crash down. But then the sky mysteriously cleared up.

Petros calmly turned to his new friends. "I am sorry. This is the way it is for me in Trellis. The kids all think I am awkward and that bad luck follows me like a black cat."

"Well, that's *silly*," Clara declared. "You are not bad luck. You've been nothing but kind to us."

Lucas put his arm around Petros's shoulder. "And anyone can outgrow clumsiness. Even me."

Petros smiled, and a ray of sun broke through the trees.

"Thanks," he said.

The friends walked all through
the city. Petros showed them the
great cathedral, the Knotted Turret,
and even the Sky Farm. Finally they
reached the edge of the city.

"Hey, that's the Witch of Bogburp's
house!" Lucas said, pointing.

Petros nodded. "Trellis sits right
in between Bogburp and Hobsgrove."

Lucas and Clara gave each other a meaningful look.

"Maybe that's why there's magic afoot in Trellis," Lucas said.

Petros's face darkened again. "Magic? What are you talking about?"

But before Lucas could answer, a horn sounded in the forest. "The knights are back! Sorry, Petros, but we have to go!"

Lucas and Clara raced back to the great oak tree lift.

"Wait!" Petros cried, stumbling after them. "I need to know why you're so worried about magic!"

But they couldn't hear him.

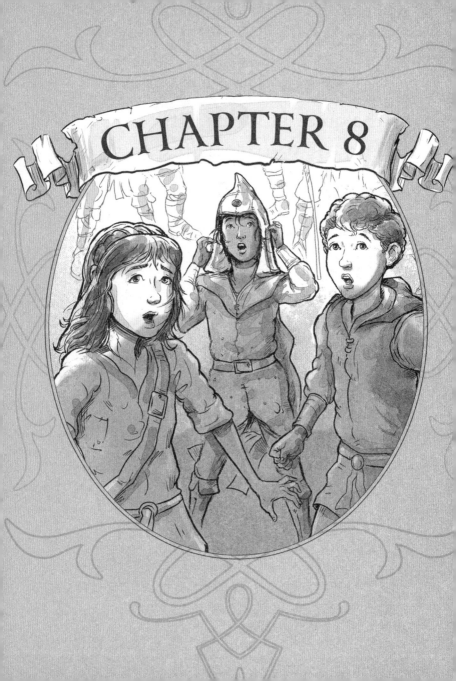

CHAPTER 8

Trellis, Beware!

Lucas and Clara waited for the wooden doors to open. The townspeople had gathered there too. Petros watched from the edge of the crowd, his face creased with worry.

All at once the large doors swung open and the knights' horses stampeded onto the street. Everyone scattered to make way for the horses, and a cry went up from the crowd.

The horses had no riders!

Then a dark, ghostly cloud swirled out from inside the great oak lift. The vapor formed into a shadow that roared an eerie warning.

Trellis be warned
    on this dark day!
Beware to ALL
    who cross my way!
If nature is what
    you seek to save,
then you must watch
    how you behave.
No hurtful words
    or calling names.
No hateful playground
    bully games.
The knights who tried
    to do some good
have now been turned
    to bark and wood.

88

Then the shadow vanished into the treetops like smoke in the air.

Lucas and Clara pushed into the tree and gasped in horror.

The knights had all been turned into statues of wood.

CHAPTER 9

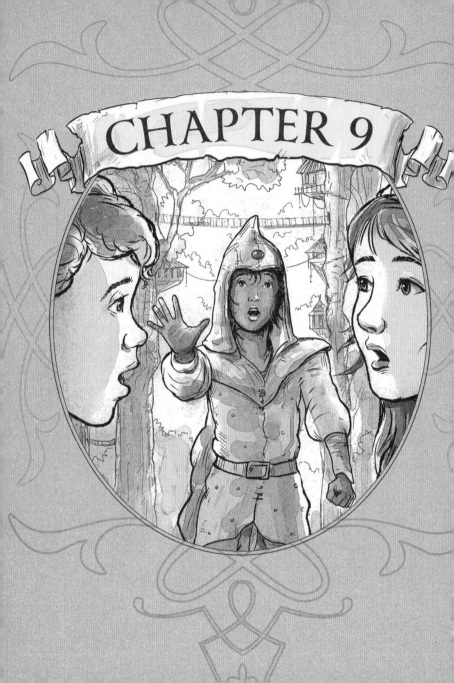

Dark Magic

"There is definitely dark magic at work here!" Lucas cried. "We'll need the help of the wizards!"

Then the prince called for a scribe to send a message to the king.

"Wait!" Petros shouted out as he beckoned wildly. "Follow me! It's important!"

As Lucas and Clara went to him, the crowd started booing and

blaming Petros, saying things like
"Evil boy, this is all your fault" and
"You've infected Trellis with some-
thing wicked."

When they were finally alone, Petros confessed, "I need your help! This whole thing *is* my fault!"

His body shook as if he had been out in the cold too long. Lucas extended a comforting hand.

"How could this possibly be your fault?" he said gently.

Clara stepped closer too. "This is sorcery, Petros. It has nothing to do with you."

But Petros backed away. "You are wrong! This has *everything* to do with me."

"What are you talking about?" Lucas asked.

Petros began to cry, and at the same time it began to rain.

"I am the *sorcerer*!" he declared. And the moment he said it, lightning flashed and thunder boomed.

A wave of fear washed over Lucas as the rain fell down in sheets.

He thought of the shadow. He thought of the wooden knights. He thought of the kids on the playground. Then he thought of how kind Petros had been to Clara and him.

"Do not worry," Lucas said as evenly as he could. "We can help."

Clara followed Lucas's lead. "Can you tell us more?"

Suddenly the rain stopped. Petros took a deep breath, then explained. "I was born with magical powers.

But I didn't know it until other kids began to make fun of me. The more upset I got, the more bad things would happen."

"Like what?" Lucas asked.

Petros tightly clenched his hands.

"Trellis began to have very strange weather. Animals fled from their homes. The birds stopped singing. The crickets stopped chirping."

Thunder rumbled overhead like a waterfall of boulders.

"But how, Petros?" Clara asked. "You're a good person."

Petros brushed his wet hair back, revealing his large ears. "Part of me *is* good. But a sorcerer's magic has both a good side and an evil side. When I get angry, the evil side of my powers begins to grow. Now my evil side has grown into a powerful, menacing shadow. And who knows what it'll do next!"

CHAPTER 10

Ghoul Duel

"There's only one thing to do!" Lucas said. "You have to control your anger, or your shadow will destroy Trellis— and possibly the entire kingdom of Wrenly!"

As soon as Lucas spoke, the shadow swooped from the clouds.

"And that is my plan!" the shadow shrieked. "I will destroy all those who have brought harm to Petros."

Lucas grabbed Petros by the shoulders and looked him in the eye. "You are the only one who can stop your shadow! Call on the good magic within you. Choose to become a sorcerer for good!"

The shadow plunged between Petros and Lucas. "He'll *never* destroy me!" it roared. "He's too full of anger! He must get revenge!"

Then the shadow reached dark tendrils out that touched Lucas and Clara. Instantly the two of them were rooted in place. Lucas looked down. Their feet had turned to wood.

"NO!" Petros shouted. He picked up a stick and pointed it at the threatening shadow.

"You can do this, Petros!" Clara cried. "You have to replace your angry thoughts with good thoughts!"

Lucas gave Clara an admiring glance. "She's right! Choose to be a sorcerer for good—the sorcerer you were meant to be! Tame the evil magic with positive feelings!"

Petros and the shadow circled each other.

"I don't have bad feelings!" Petros began. "I only have *good* feelings."

The shadow laughed mockingly. "You're more foolish than I thought! You're nothing but a sniveling outcast, and you *know it*! Nobody wants you here."

Petros staggered at the insult.

"That's *not true*!" Lucas shouted as the curse moved upward, turning his chest into wood. "You have the gift of magic! Use your power to help Trellis, not destroy it. You are good."

Petros fought back harder this time. "I do have a gift! And my gift is *goodness*! My gift is *forgiveness*! My gift is *understanding* and *love*!"

The shadow cringed and faded at the declarations. Petros saw the effect his good thoughts were having. He fought even harder.

"I have the power to think and act rightly!" Petros shouted. "I am a force for good! You are *nothing* but anger and fear. Your dark thoughts are no part of me. Be gone!"

At this, the shadow turned into a thin film of smoke and was drawn into the stick Petros was holding.

"No-o-o-o-o-o!" it wailed pathetically. "You cannot destroy me! I am hatred! I am anger! I am *real*!"

But the shadow's voice had grown weak and faint.

"I am *stronger* than you!" Petros roared. "My power is for *good*. You don't scare me anymore."

When the shadow had vanished into the stick, Petros held it high and snapped it in half. Sunshine erupted through the clouds.

"You did it!" Lucas and Clara cried. The curse was broken, and they could move again.

"I am a new person," Petros said. "I feel happy and free."

All through the forest the birds sang in the trees. Rabbits hopped into their holes. Bears toddled to their dens. Everything returned to normal.

"You *are* free!" Lucas said. "And

so is Trellis! Now let's check on the
knights!"

The children made their way to
the great oak lift. The knights were
inside—alive and well. They rubbed
their eyes as if waking from a sound
sleep.

"What happened here?" asked Sir Desdan, scratching his head.

"The curse has been lifted," Lucas said.

The bearded knight raised an eyebrow. "Defeated by the likes of you children?"

"Not us," Lucas said. "The evil shadow was defeated by someone pure of heart and full of hope."

Then, in front of the crowd of villagers, Lucas took Petros's hand and lifted it up. "Today Trellis has found a hero. I give you Petros the Sorcerer, defender of all things good in the wood."

And everyone in the crowd roared
with approval.

Enter

The Kingdom of Wrenly

For more books, excerpts, and activities, visit **KingdomofWrenly.com**!